The Last Tree

Emily Haworth-Booth

PAVILION

Once upon a time, a group of friends
were looking for a place to live.

The desert was too hot,

the valley was too wet,

The Last Tree

For Rose and Grace, who bring the garden to life

With thanks to
Clémence Viel, Rachel Stubbs,
Chris Petrie, Sophie Herxheimer,
Neil Dunnicliffe, Hattie Grylls, Dax Rossetti
and Alice, Rosie and Mark Haworth-Booth
who helped to grow and prune this book.

First published in the UK in 2020 by Pavilion Books Company Limited,
43 Great Ormond Street, London WC1N 3HZ

Publisher: Neil Dunnicliffe • Editor: Harriet Grylls
Designed by Emily Haworth-Booth and Anna Lubecka

ISBN: 9781843654377 • A CIP catalogue record for this book is
available from the British Library. • 10 9 8 7 6 5 4 3 2 1

Reproduction by Mission Production Ltd., Hong Kong
Printed by Toppan Leefung Ltd., China

This book can be ordered from the publisher online at www.pavilionbooks.com, or try your local bookshop.

MIX
Paper from
responsible sources
FSC® C104723

To find out more about trees and how to plant them, visit www.treesforcities.org and www.woodlandtrust.org.uk

and the mountain was too windy.

Nowhere was quite right
until they saw the first tree...

...and came to the forest, where dappled light fell through the leaves and a gentle breeze twisted between the branches.

All summer long the friends lived and played among the trees and slept on the mossy floor.

When winter came, the breeze turned colder, and they took a few branches for firewood.

But where they had taken branches, the rain came through and put out their fires.

They chopped down a few whole trees to build shelters, but that made the forest colder still.

So they cut down some more trees to turn their shelters into cabins.

Soon it seemed that the more wood they took, the more they needed to take.

When summer returned, the sun blazed down and there weren't enough trees left to shade them. Yet a few more branches made very pleasant porches.

Before long the people became skilled carpenters, and all summer they worked hard to make the perfect village.

Porches for shade

Ladders for climbing up to build porches

Laundry poles

Laundry pole ornaments

Chairs for sitting under porches

Carpentry tables

Rulers for making things straight

Wooden sculptures to look at

But when the autumn winds came through again, they whipped through the spaces where the trees used to be, throwing all the villagers' fine work into disarray.

They needed a new plan.
One that would solve all their problems, forever.

And with the wood they built a wall.

What fun they had working together to build it,
and how proud they were when it was done!

Stillness descended like a blanket. The clothes stayed put.
The plants grew tall and straight. At last, the place really was just right.

But with nothing to look at but the wall,
something happened to the people, too.

In time they started to forget their games and songs,
and soon the happy village had grown cold and hard,
for now the villagers had walls around their hearts.

It had taken all the wood they had to build the wall...

...and so before too long, each parent, thinking they were being clever, said the same thing to their child:

But when the children,

creeping out beyond the wall,

found each other by the little tree,

they soon forgot their task.

They laughed

and ran

and played

and sang

and tended the tree

and gathered its seeds.

Each day they visited,

it grew a little taller and more proud –

until they knew that they could never cut the last tree down.

Meanwhile, each night the parents asked their children why they hadn't brought back wood. But when the children talked about the tree and how it made them feel, their parents wouldn't come outside to look, or even listen.

That's when the children knew what they had to do. They started to bring home wood, but it wasn't from the last tree.

And when it was delivered, plank by plank, their parents didn't question why it was so long and straight and smooth. All they said was "This'll do just fine," and "Oh, that's good!"

They boarded and banged and fenced and reinforced
and never once looked out or up.

It was only when the wind rushed into the village,

rattling their boarded-up windows

and knocking down their new fences

that they ran outside and saw that despite all their new wood...

...the last tree still stood.

In the bright daylight
they remembered
that they were old
friends, not enemies.

And when they heard their
children playing in the tree,

saw how the cool
wind twisted gently
through its branches

and the sunshine fell
in dappled shadows to
the ground beneath,

they were reminded of
how things used to be.

Then all at once they
understood what
they had done

and how, perhaps,
they could begin again.

What fun they had taking down the wall,
and how proud they were when it was done!

As they planted seeds and tended the saplings,
they talked and sang, and as the children grew
a new forest grew with them...

...and the last tree became the first.